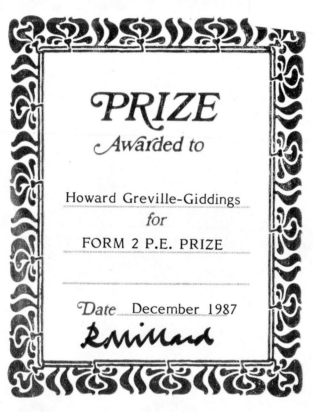

PRIZE

Awarded to

Howard Greville-Giddings

for

FORM 2 P.E. PRIZE

Date December 1987

PHILIP & TACEY LTD Andover Hants   Ref. 048-003-000

I'm afraid of monsters,
particularly those
with large amounts of curly hair
growing from their toes.

It's not so much the hairy bits
that frighten me to death,
it's more the thought of feeling
a monster's hairy breath.

Monsters can look curious,
especially when they're small.
Little tufts of hair grow where
you have none at all.

And when they grow up bigger,
some parts of them grow long.
In fact, so elongated
you'd think they don't belong.

I think that monsters eat a lot,
all kinds of different food.
What seems to me quite horrible,
a monster will think good.

To fill a monster's appetite,
a garden full of flowers
wouldn't last for half a day,
as monsters munch for hours.

Nothing that a monster eats
are things that you would like.
They even like their meals on wheels,
so I always hide my bike.

Imagine how a monster's mouth
would deal with chains and spokes,
and how the bell would tickle
as it vanished down its throat.

The problem with most monsters
is they hardly make a sound,
at least not in a language
that I can understand.

They creep and crawl and shuffle
and creak through every door,
and then they slide and slither
across the bedroom floor.

I find it most disturbing
to go upstairs alone.
I know it may seem silly
when Mum and Dad are home.

But there's a little voice in me
that tells me not to look,
in case I see or touch something
that's crept out from a book.

It might look like a rabbit,
but I'm sensible enough
to think of all the monsters
with fangs as well as fluff.

I'm afraid that monsters
are cleverer than cats.
Their tails are so much longer
and they use them just like bats.

Outside they try to look like
the washing on the line,
but then they wave their arms about
and start a clumsy climb.

They seem to climb quite oddly,
their heads some way behind,
while out in front their toes will curl
round anything they find.

Some monsters can be friendly,
surprising as it seems,
quiet as mice and smiling,
having pleasant dreams.

So boys and girls be careful
when monsters seem asleep.
Although their toes are twitching,
their dreams may not be deep.

But monsters have a funny way
of sometimes being kind,
especially when I lie awake
with monsters on my mind.

Instead of pouncing on the bed
and tugging at my ears,
monsters seem to melt away
and then they disappear.

In fact I really think I will
stop saying I'm afraid.
I'll think instead of good things
that monsters do and say.

Like monsters munching sandwiches
and leaving me the crumbs,
or monsters giving parties
and dancing on their thumbs.

My Dad says monsters only live
where children fear to go,
so if you're wise, you'll realise
it's best to shout "hello".

It's simply that a monster
is just like you or me.
It never likes to be surprised
by things it cannot see.